Goose
Moon

by
Carolyn Arden

Illustrated by
Jim Postier

Boyds Mills Press

Published by Boyds Mills Press, Inc.
A Highlights Company
815 Church Street
Honesdale, Pennsylvania 18431
Printed in China
Visit our Web site at www.boydsmillspress.com

Publisher Cataloging-in-Publication Data (U.S.)

Arden, Carolyn.
Goose moon / by Carolyn Arden ; illustrated by Jim Postier.
—1st ed.
[32] p. : col. ill. ;   cm.
Summary: A young girl anxiously waits the arrival of spring to
see the Goose Moon, a sign that spring is on its way.
ISBN 1-59078-040-X
1. Spring—Fiction. 2. Moon—Fiction.
I. Postier, Jim, ill. II. Title
[E] 21   PZ7.A733Go 2004
2003108161

The text of this book is set in 14-point Optima.
The illustrations are done in watercolor.

First edition, 2004

10 9 8 7 6 5 4 3 2

To Grampa Dyce,
whose love of nature inspired me,
and to my parents,
who encouraged us to explore.
—C. A.

For my friends Laurie, Steve, and Vicki.
Special thanks to Aubrey
and Grandpa Bob
—J. P.

Winter is coming.

I know because Grampa and I saw the geese fly away today. They gathered in the field, honking and flapping their creaky wings, then rose up into the air. "Wait for me!" I shouted as I ran beneath them.

I closed my eyes and imagined myself going with them, flying over rivers and mountains to a place that was warm and sunny. But when I opened my eyes, a cold wind was blowing and the geese were gone.

The next morning, there is glittery frost on my window. I make a foggy circle on the glass with my warm breath and draw a picture on it.

At school that day, we are just finishing our show and tell when the teacher stops. "Look!" she says. "It's snowing." We all crowd to the window to watch the big, soft flakes floating down.

Winter is fun. We have snowball fights and climb huge drifts of snow. We snap icicles off the barn and lick them like ice pops. We go tobogganing in the woods and have big pileups at the bottom of the hill.

At night, we sit by the cozy fire with mugs of hot cocoa. Grampa plays the guitar and we all sing "Frosty the Snowman."

But after a while, I get tired of putting on my hat, mittens, scarf, snowpants, boots, and jacket—just to go outside. I get tired of sitting inside every night. I even get tired of all the snow.

I want to chase fireflies and feel the grass tickle my bare feet. I want to pick berries and swing in the hammock. I want to jump into the cool river and look for colorful rocks on the bottom.

"Will it ever be summer again?" I ask Grampa one evening when we're doing a puzzle together. "Of course it will," he says. "But we have to be patient. We have to wait for the Goose Moon."

"What's the Goose Moon?" I ask him.

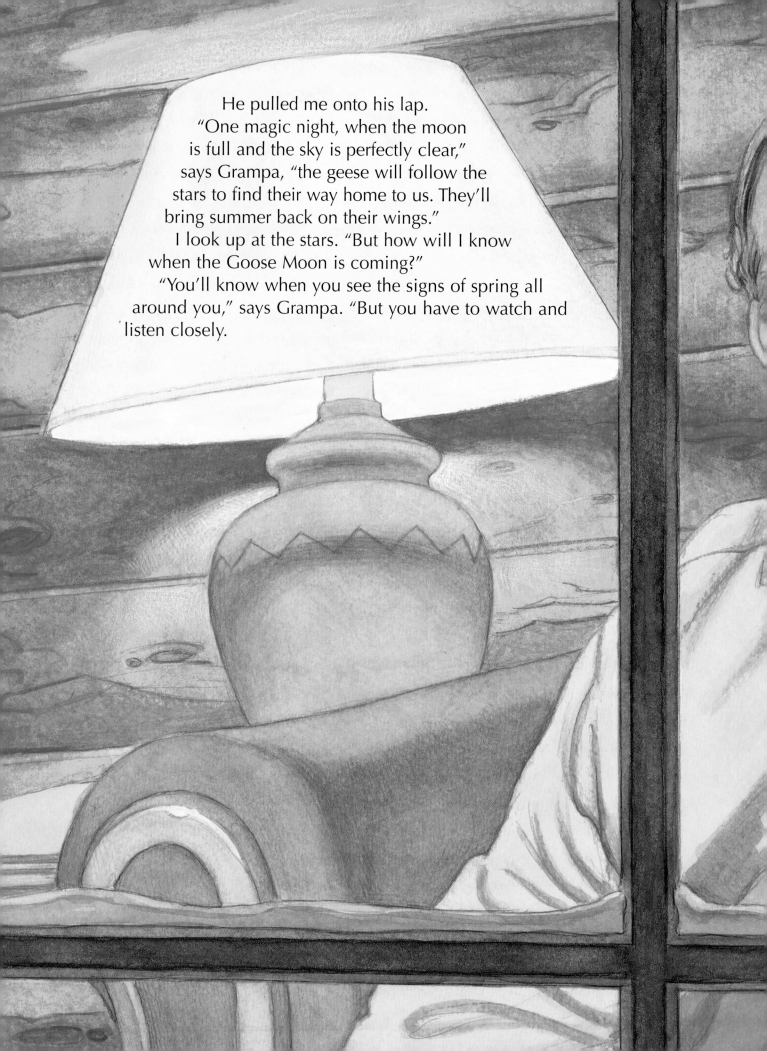

He pulled me onto his lap.
"One magic night, when the moon
is full and the sky is perfectly clear,"
says Grampa, "the geese will follow the
stars to find their way home to us. They'll
bring summer back on their wings."
I look up at the stars. "But how will I know
when the Goose Moon is coming?"
"You'll know when you see the signs of spring all
around you," says Grampa. "But you have to watch and
listen closely.

"Maybe you'll notice that the birds are singing louder each morning. Or that suddenly there's more mud under your feet than snow. You might feel a warm breeze blowing through your hair when you're playing outside. Then you'll know the Goose Moon is coming and summer can't be far behind."

Every day, I search for the signs of spring. I stop on my way home from school to watch the icicles dripping off the roof of the barn. I bend down to touch little shoots of green grass poking through the snow. I stand very still on the porch in the morning and listen to the birds.

Every night before I go to bed, I look up at the sky to see if the Goose Moon is there. Sometimes the sky is filled with stars. Sometimes there's a bright sliver of a moon peeking through the trees. And sometimes there's nothing there at all.

One night, I dream that I am a goose. We all swim together in a cool green pond, then climb out to sit on a big, warm rock with our feathers spread out to dry in the sun. I'm shaking my feathers out, watching tiny droplets of water fly into the air, when I realize that someone is gently shaking my arm.

It's Grampa. The light from my window is so bright, I have to cover my eyes. Grampa is holding my jacket. "Wake up, honeybunch," he whispers. "I want to show you something special."

We tiptoe downstairs and step out onto the front porch. It's so cold, my breath fogs. I look up and gasp. A giant, glowing moon hangs low in the sky like a big white beach ball. It is late at night, but I can see everything in the yard. Grampa squeezes my hand.

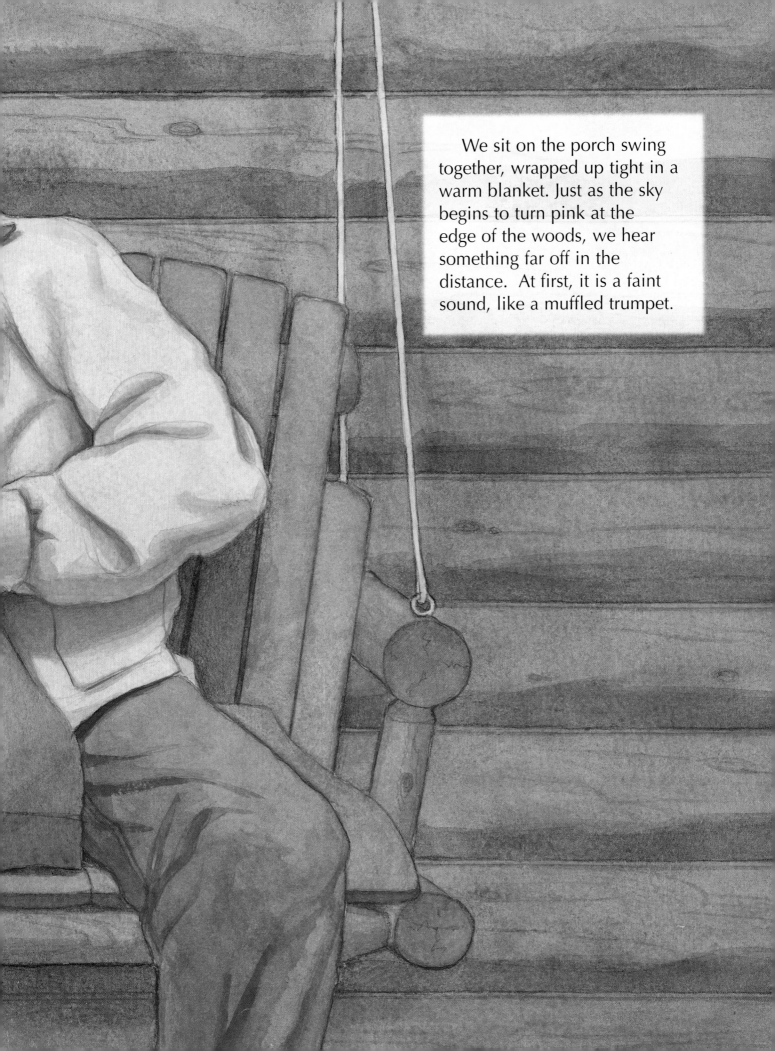

We sit on the porch swing together, wrapped up tight in a warm blanket. Just as the sky begins to turn pink at the edge of the woods, we hear something far off in the distance. At first, it is a faint sound, like a muffled trumpet.

Then it gets louder and louder. "Honk, Honk, HO-O-NK!"
A flurry of dark wings flaps across the glowing moon.

I look up at Grampa and smile.
Summer is coming.

Author's Note

The inspiration for *Goose Moon* came from Native American folklore. Many Native American tribes marked the passage of time by assigning names to each full moon of the year, creating their own lunar calendars. Some moons represented food to be harvested: the Strawberry Moon rose in June for the Chippewa and the Rice Moon came in September for the Ojibwa. Other lunar names reflected seasonal changes in the environment: the Moon of the Falling Leaves rose in November for the Sioux; the Moon When the Geese Come Home symbolized February and the beginning of spring for the Omaha.